The INSPECTOR

STEINBERG

The INSPECTOR

The Viking Press   New York

First published in 1973 by The Viking Press, Inc.
625 Madison Avenue, New York, N.Y. 10022
Published simultaneously in Canada by
The Macmillan Company of Canada Limited
SBN 670-39922-1
Library of Congress catalog card number: 72-84265
Printed in U.S.A.

Most of these drawings originally appeared in *The New Yorker*

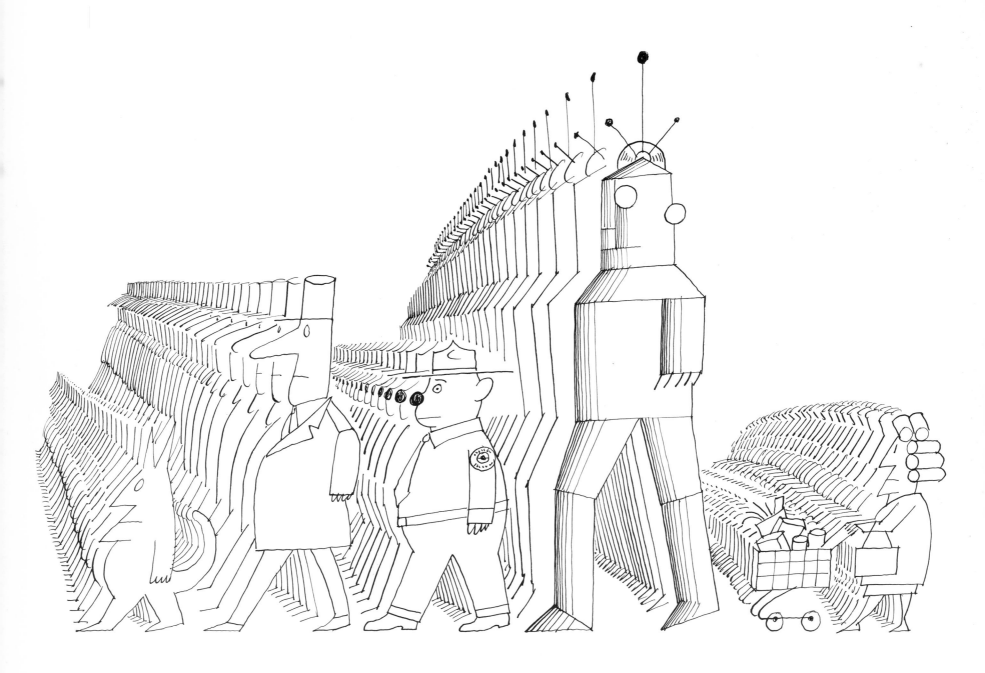

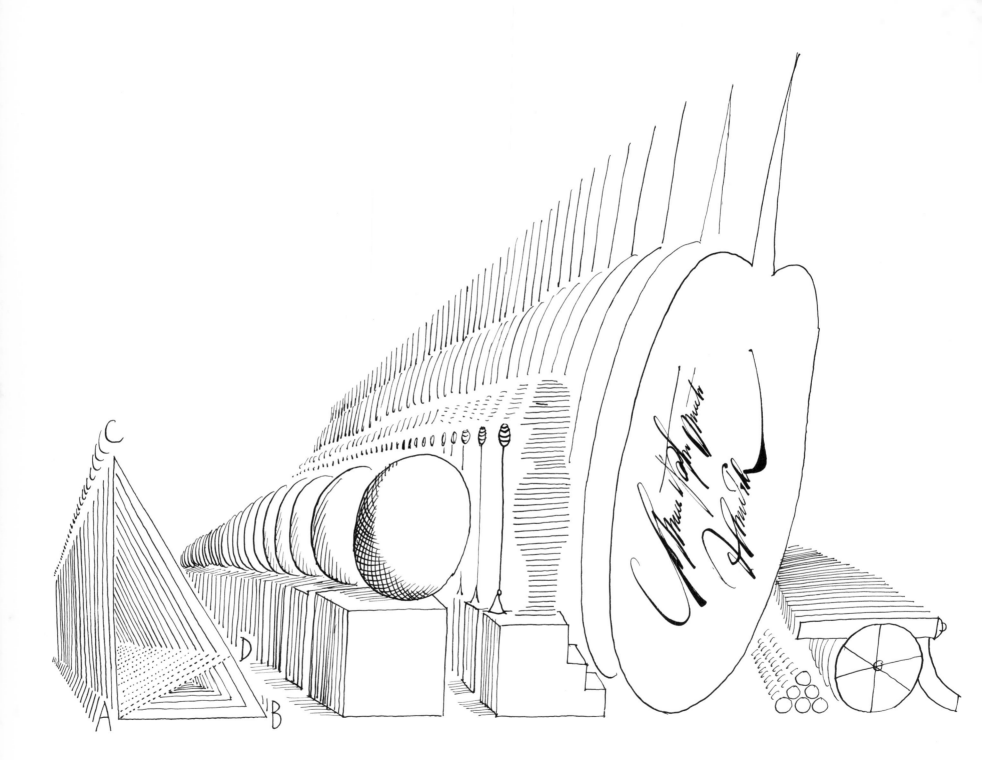

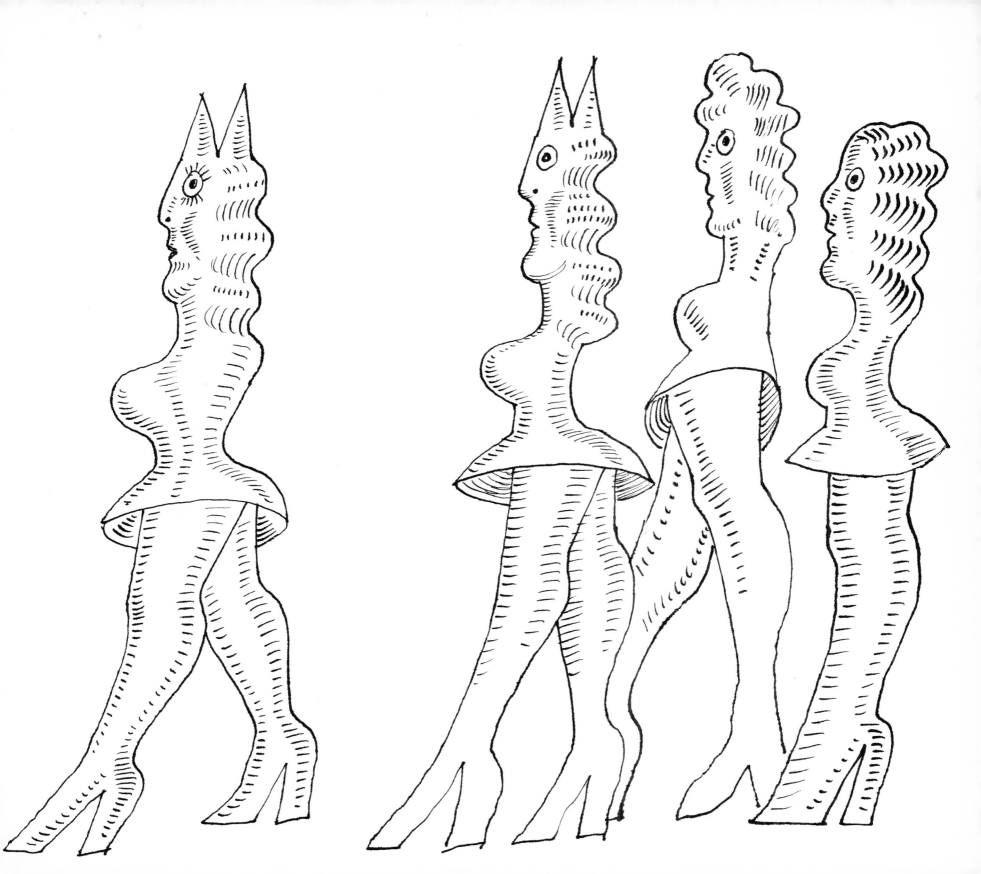

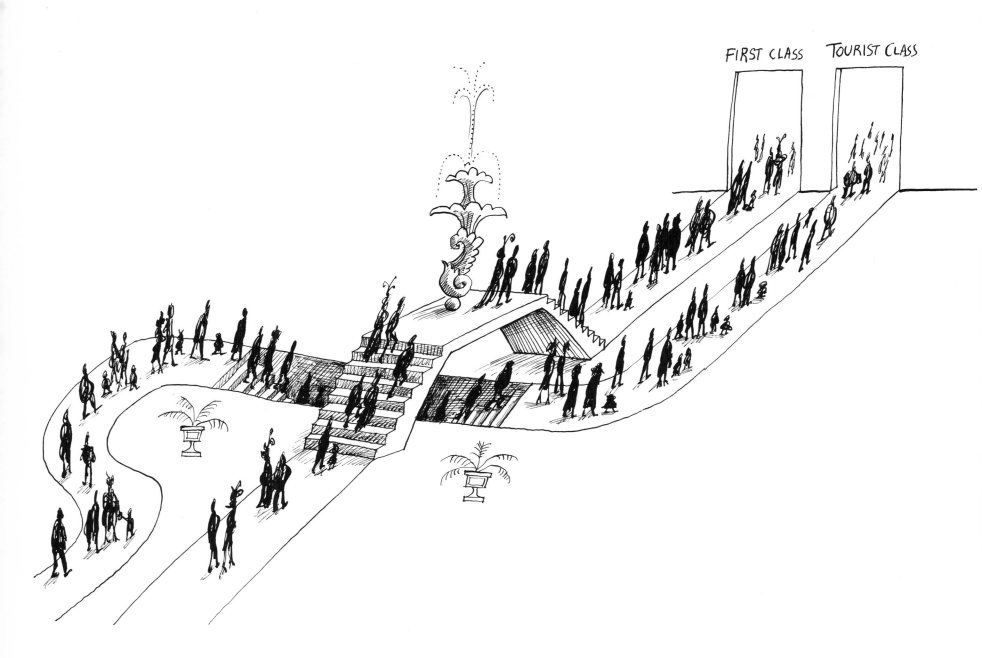

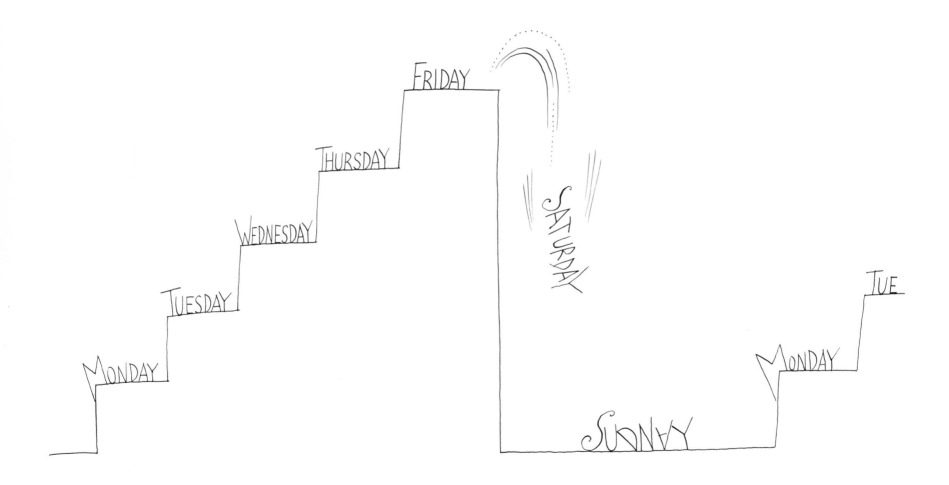

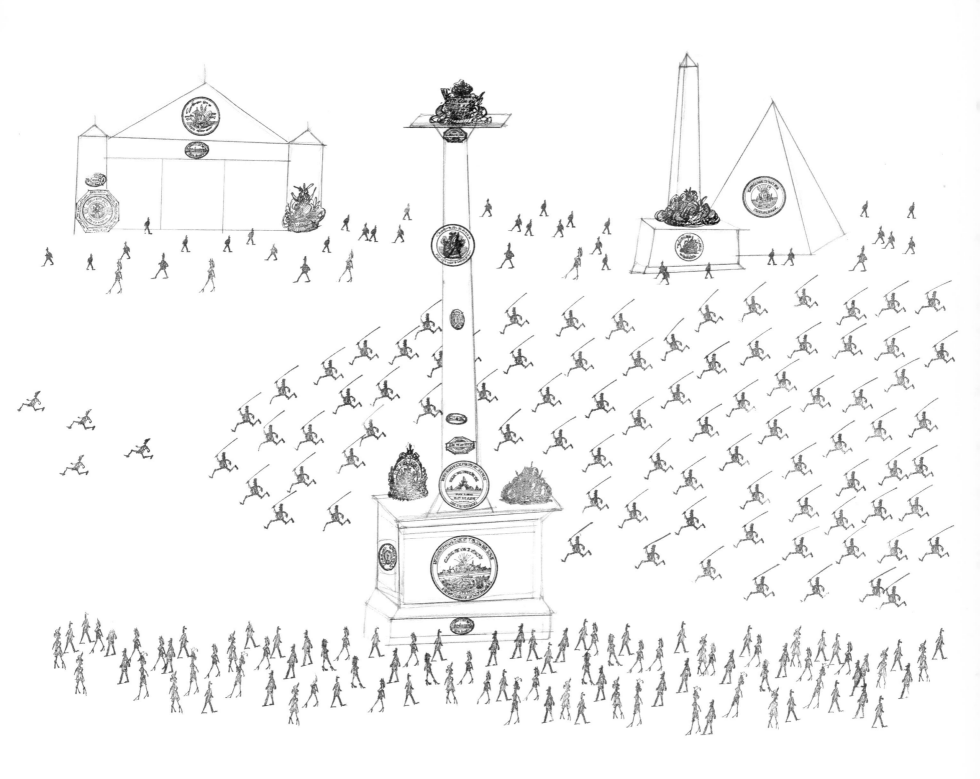

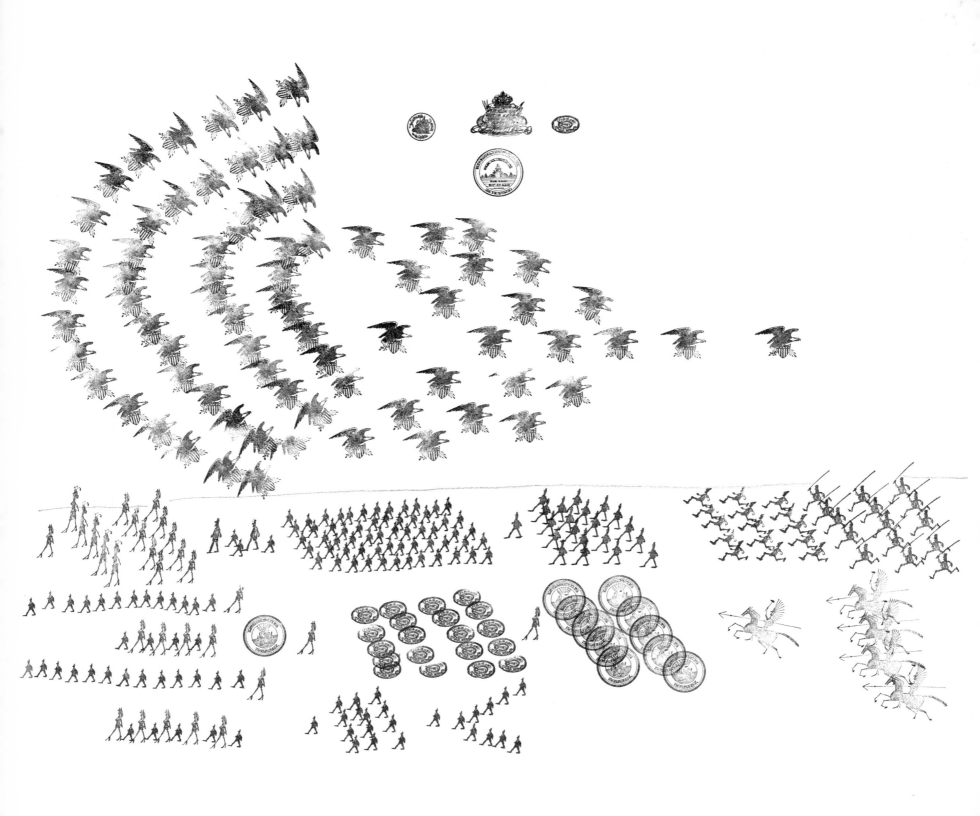

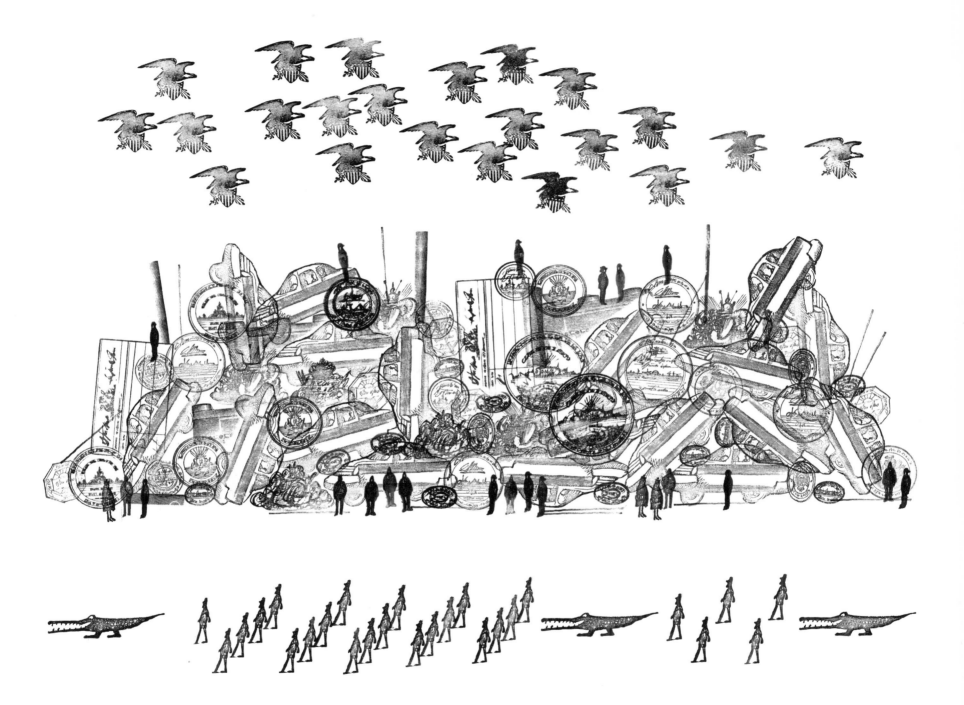

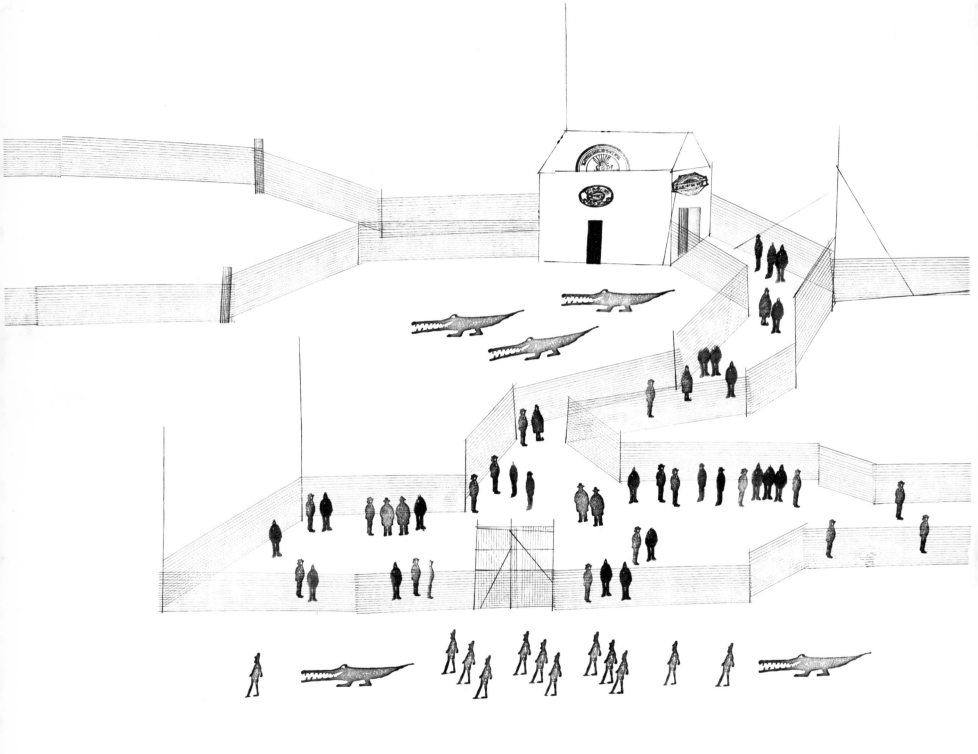

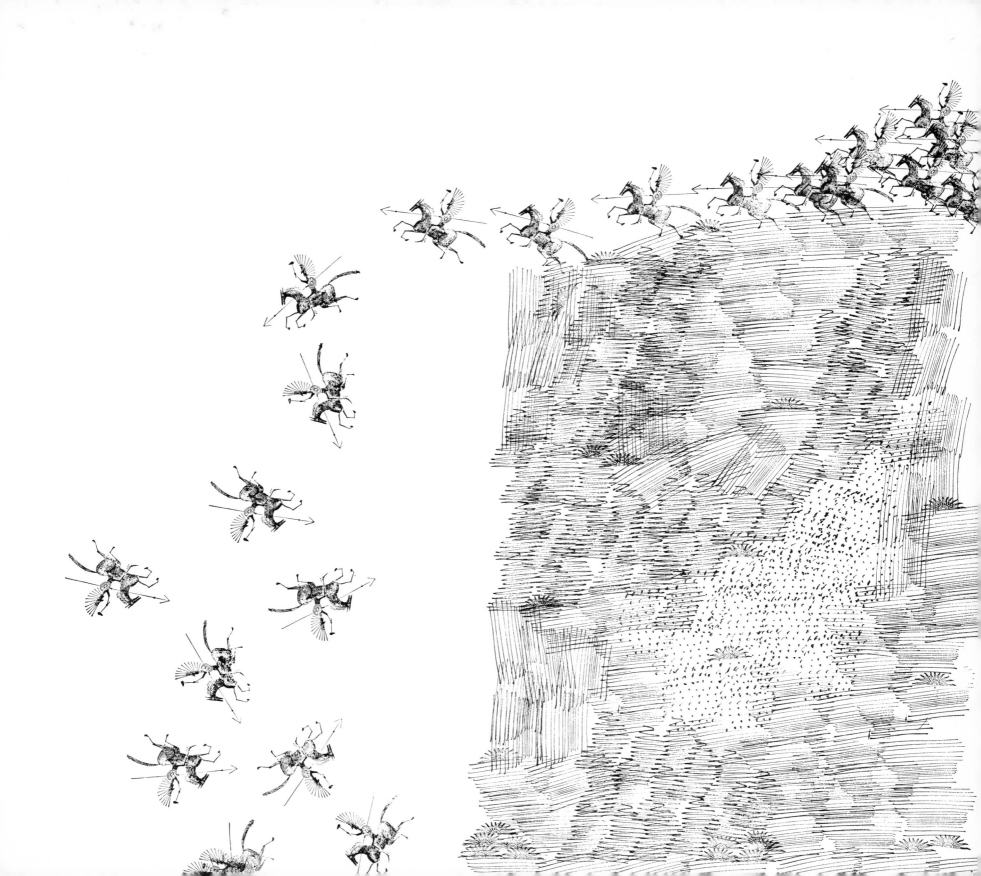

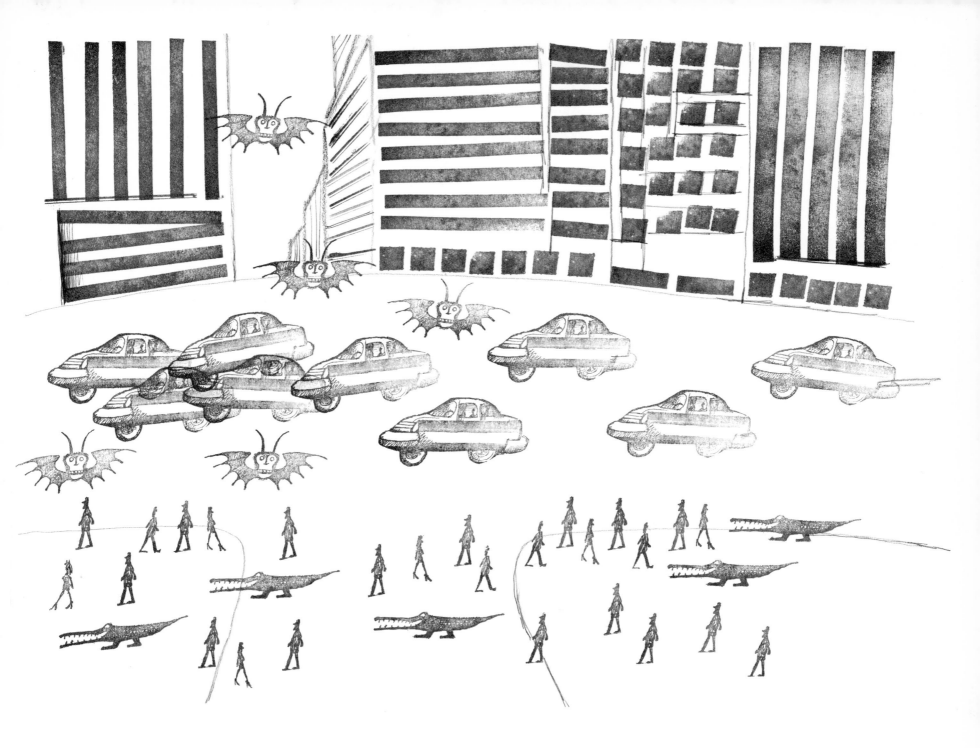

Detroit and Canada Tunnel, near American Portal, Detroit, Mich. 26

Photo Courtesy of Holden, McKinney & Clark

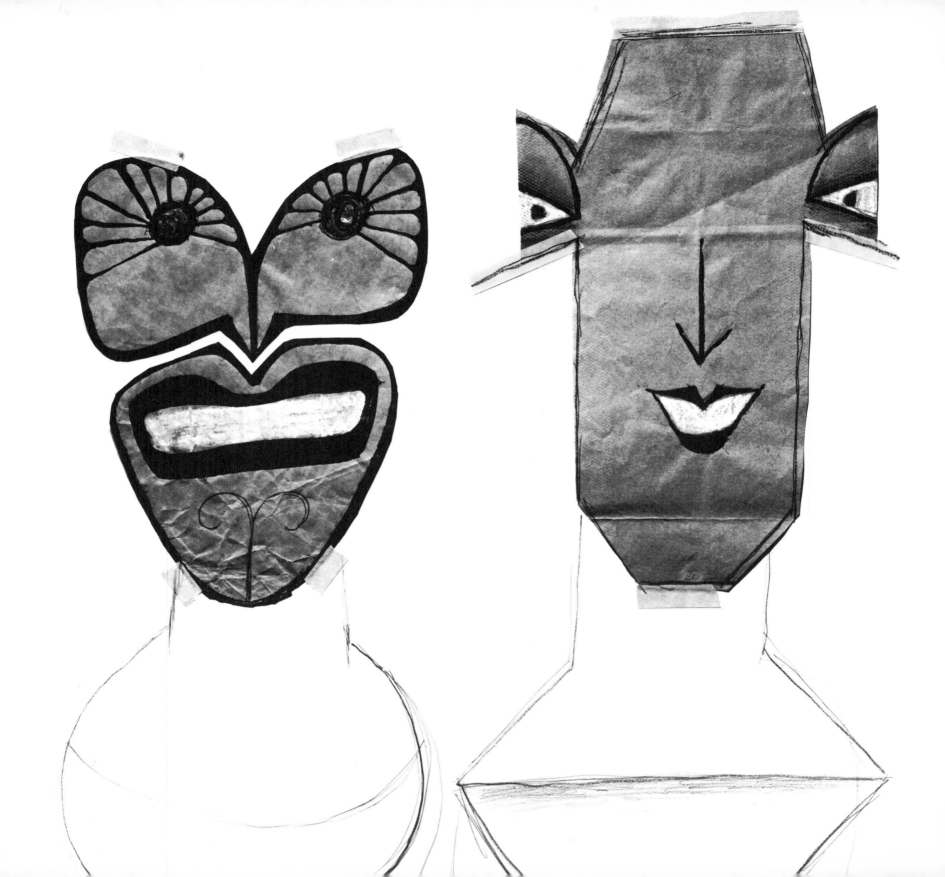

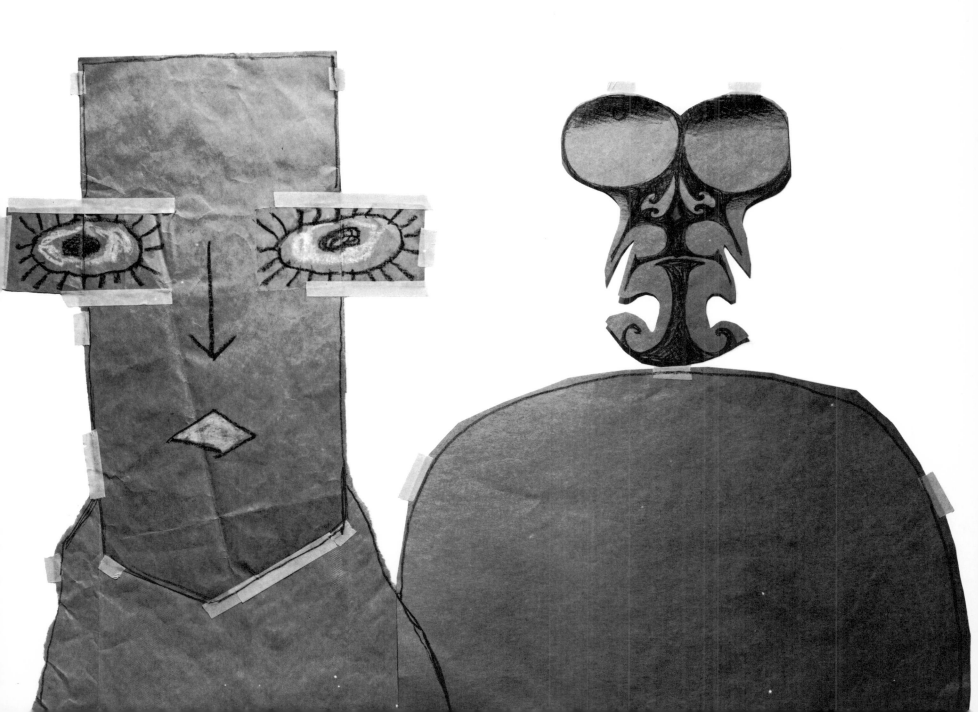

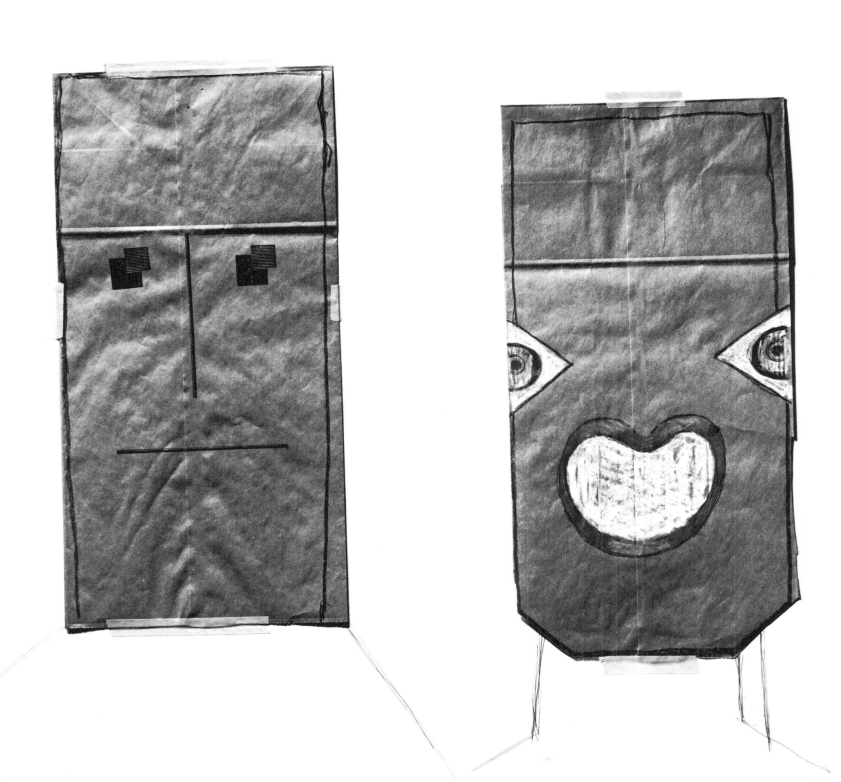

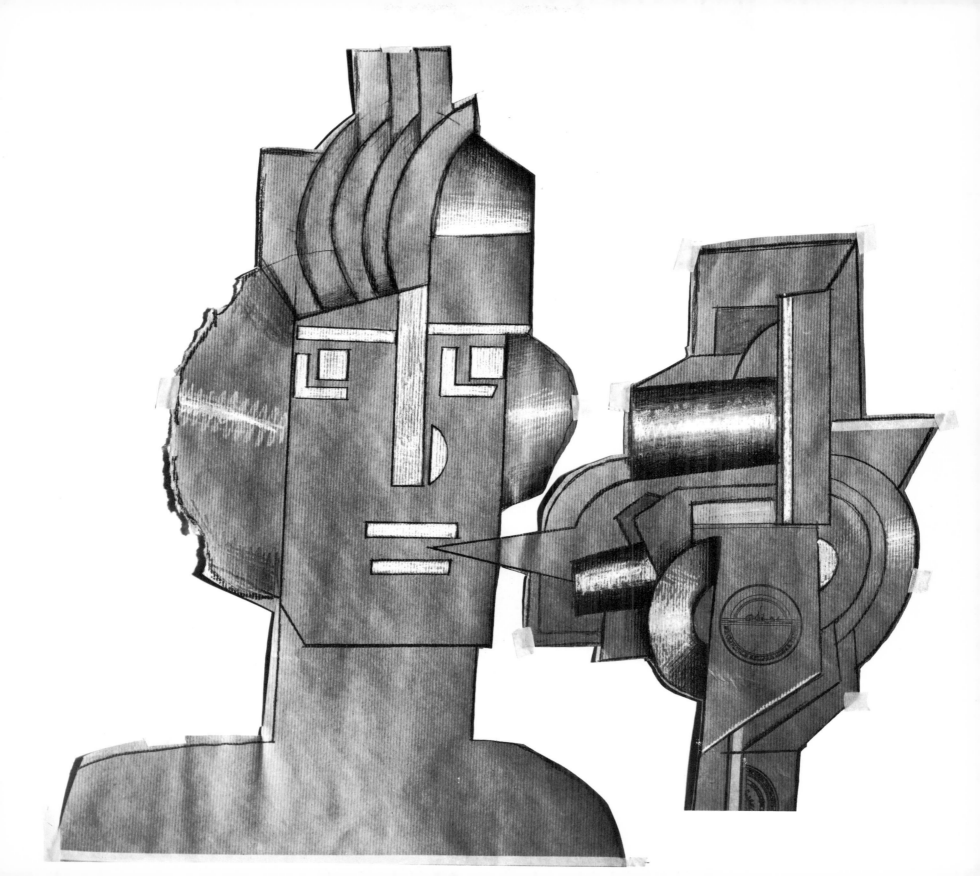

STEINBERG
1966

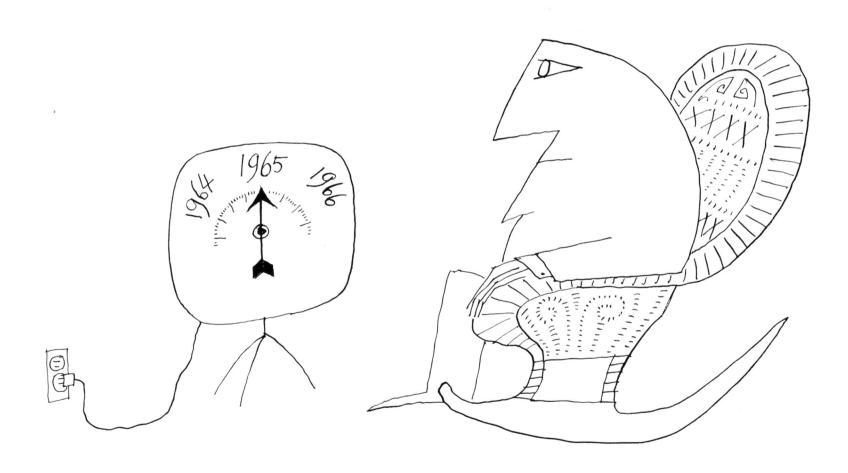

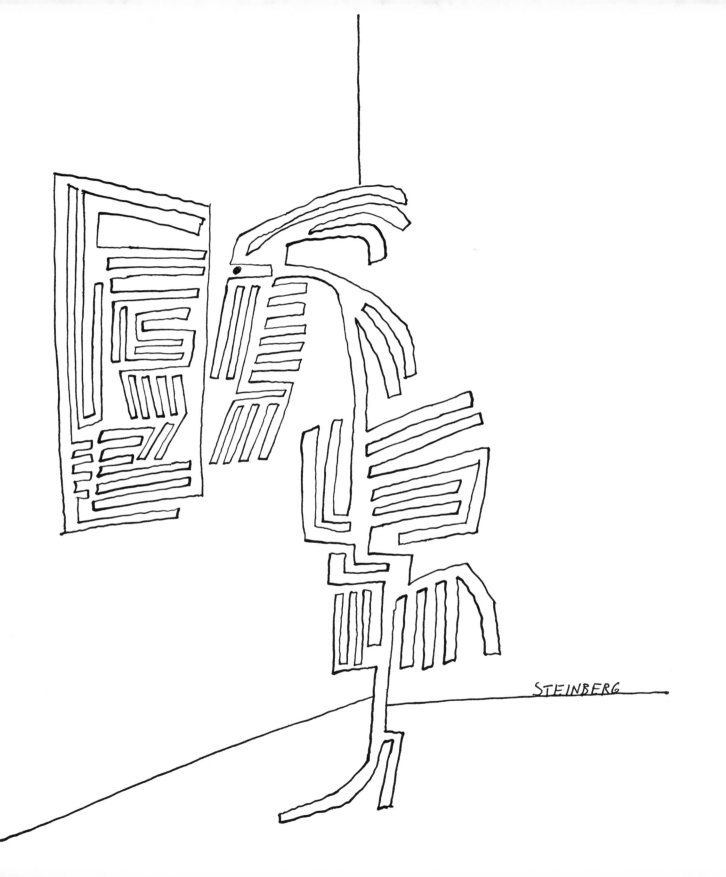

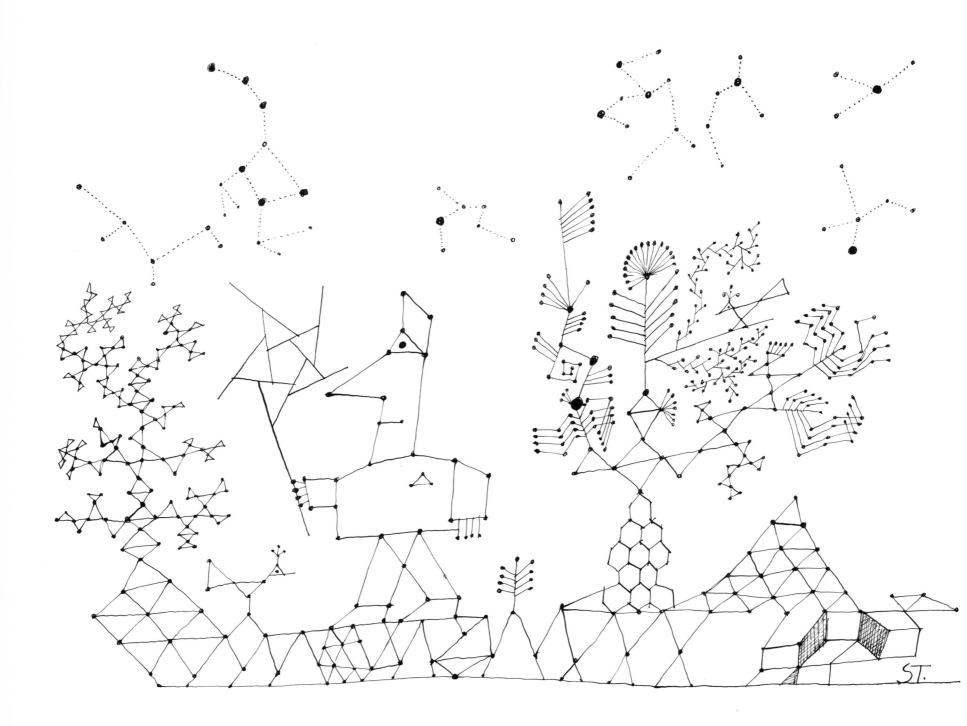

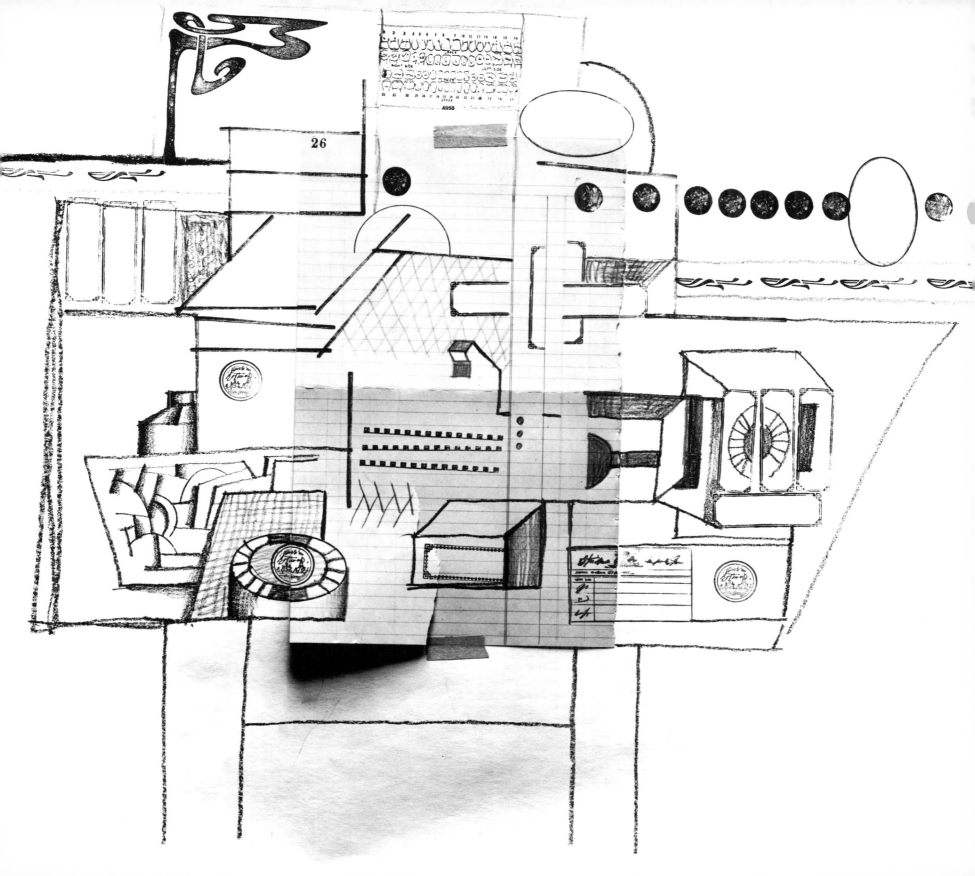

STEINBERG
68

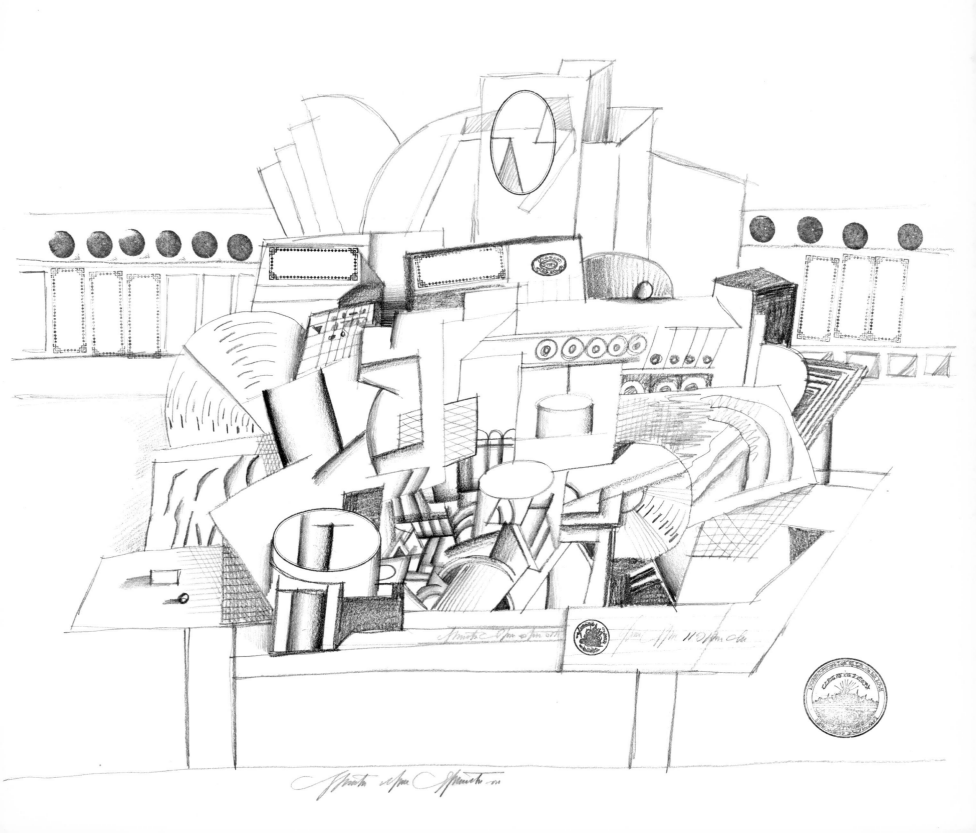

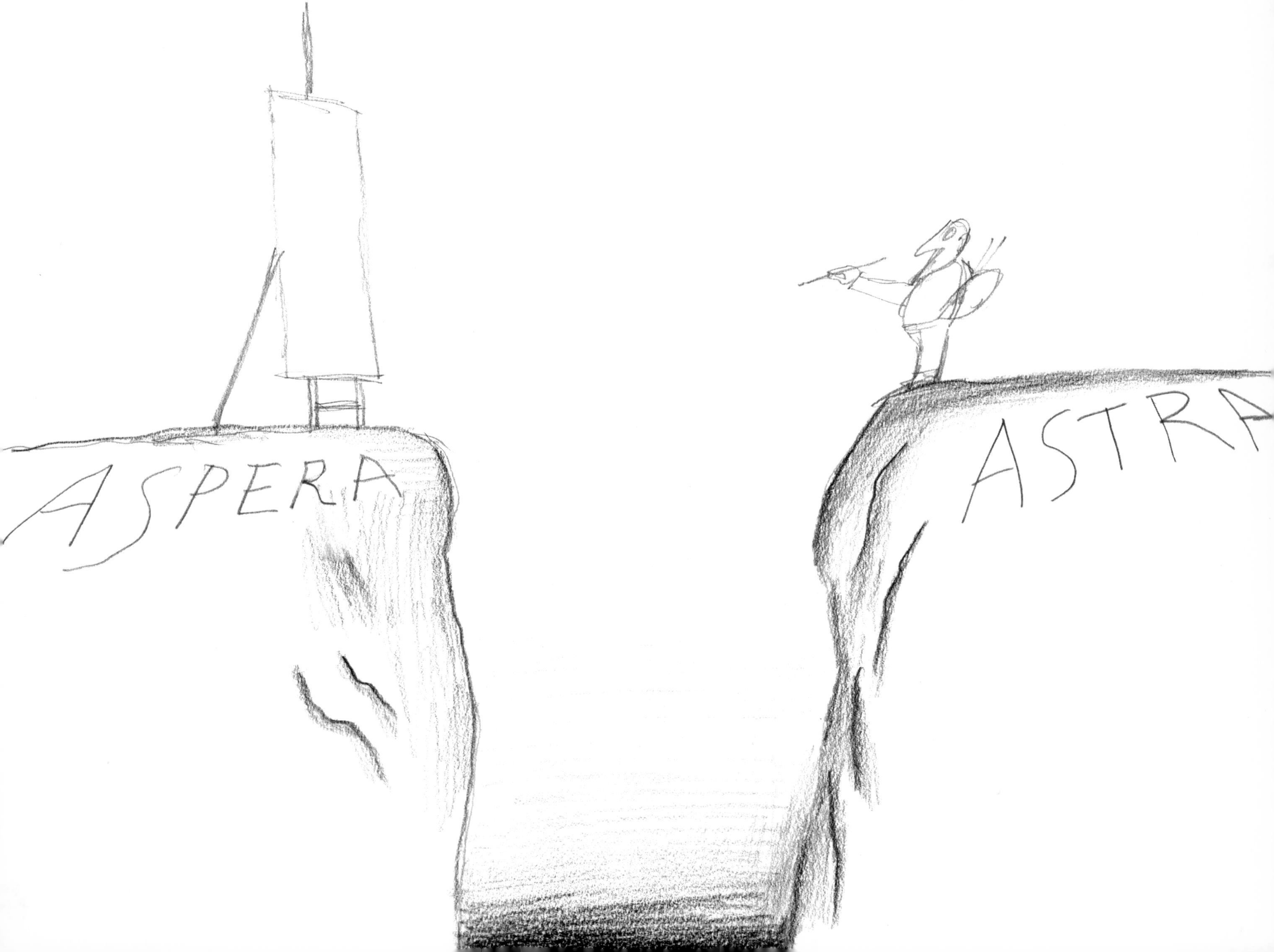
ASPERA
ASTRA

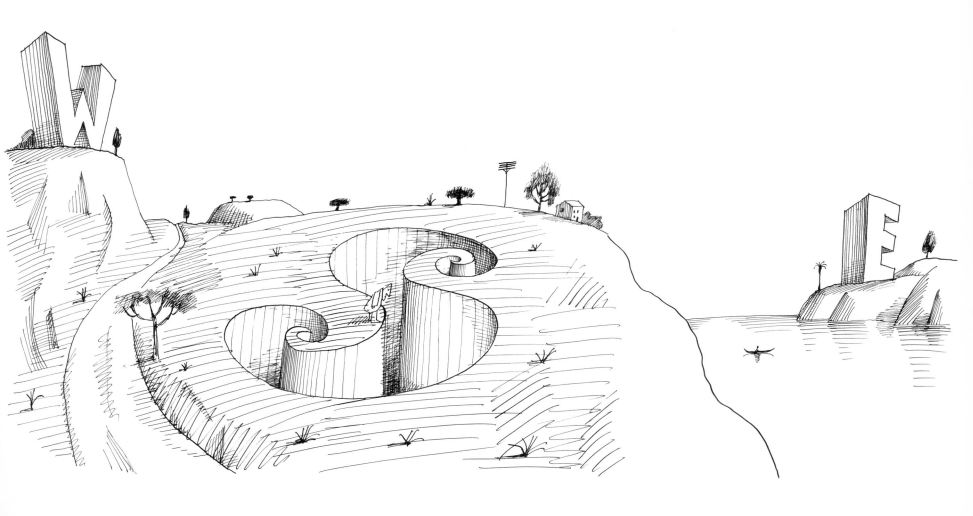

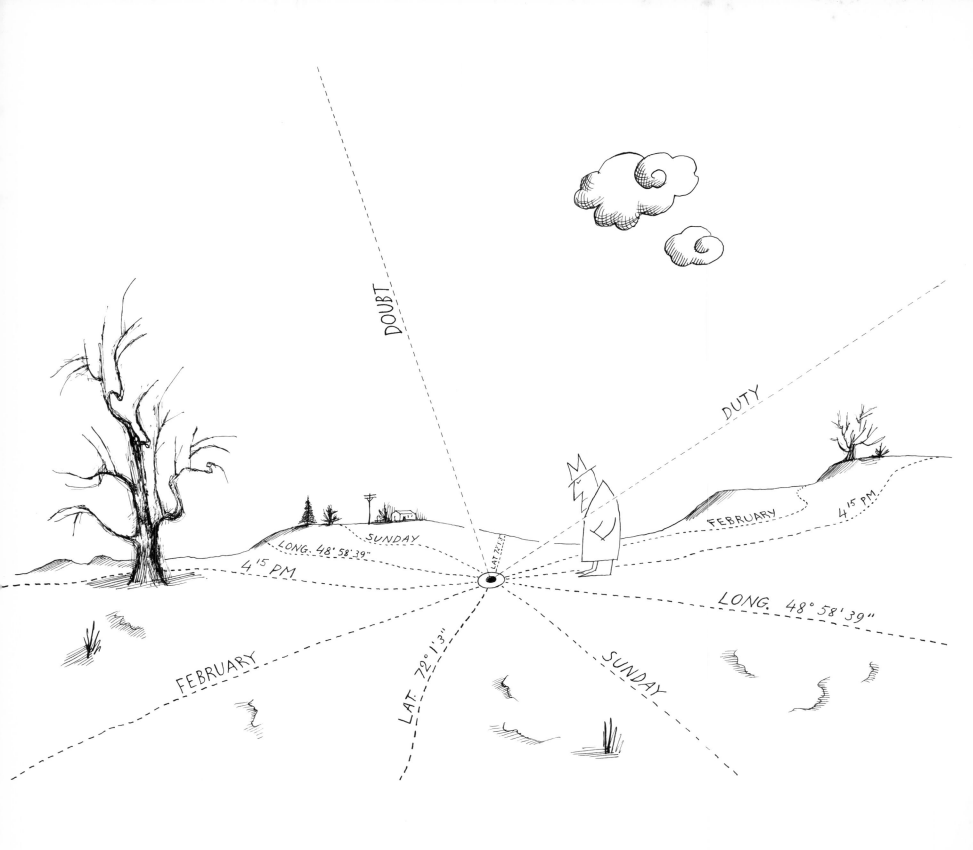

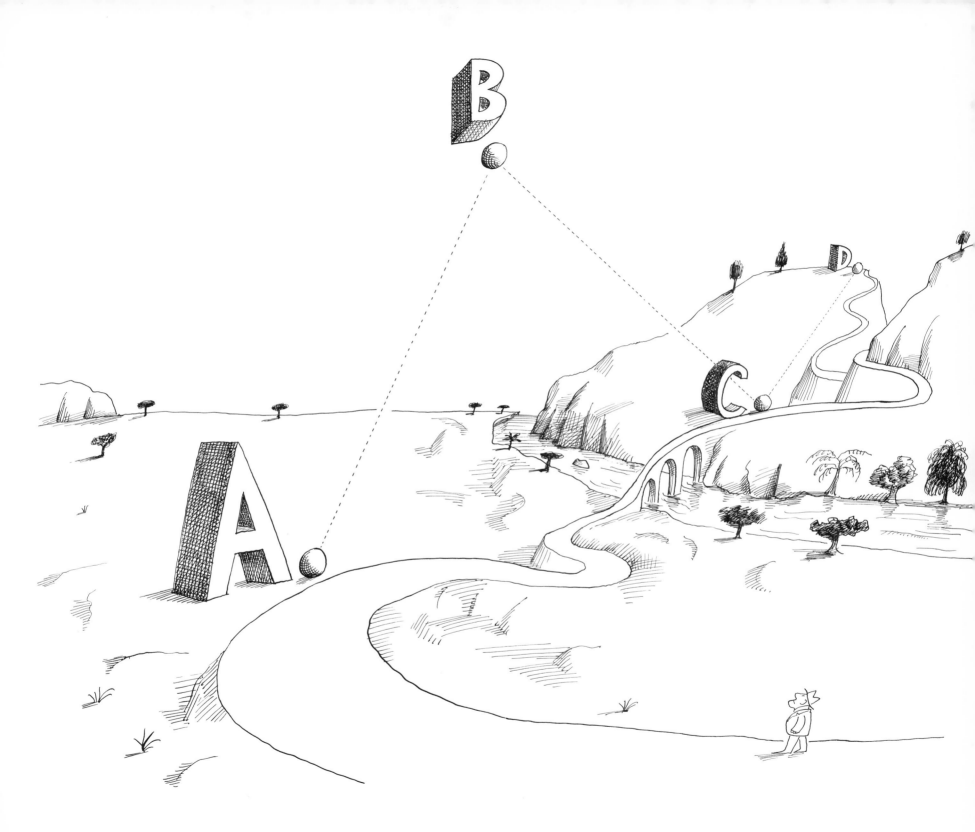

Atlantic

CANADA

New York

Chicago

San Francisco

MEXICO

Pacific

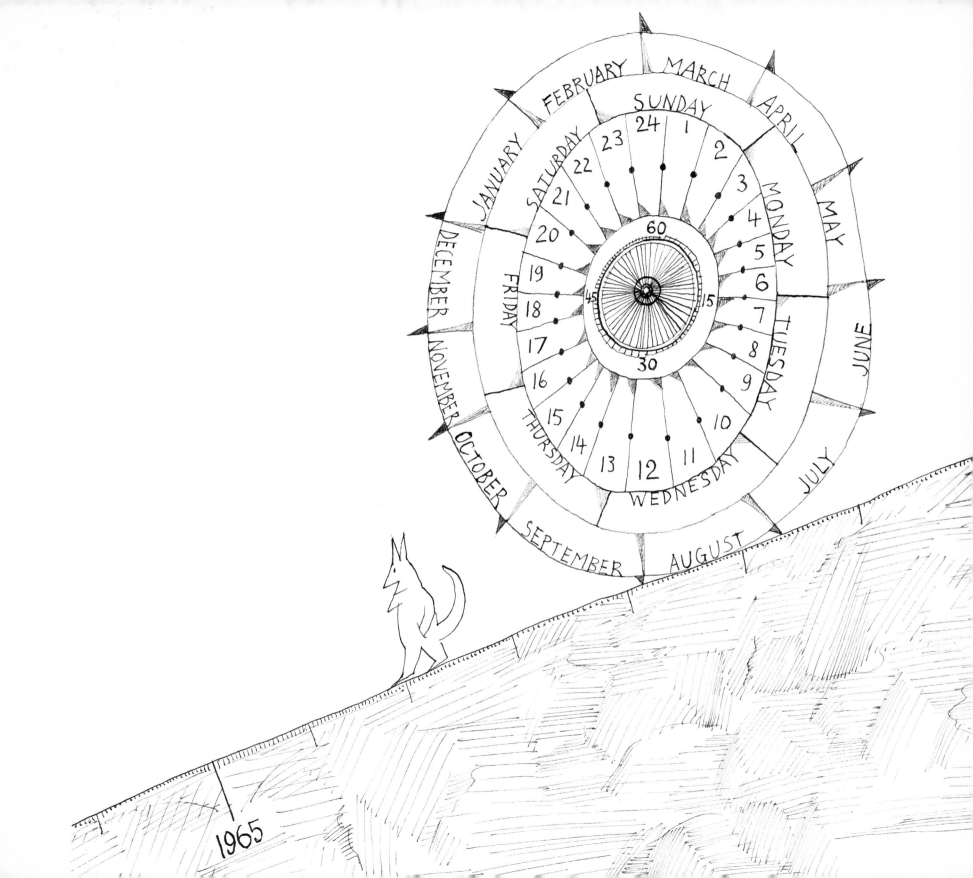

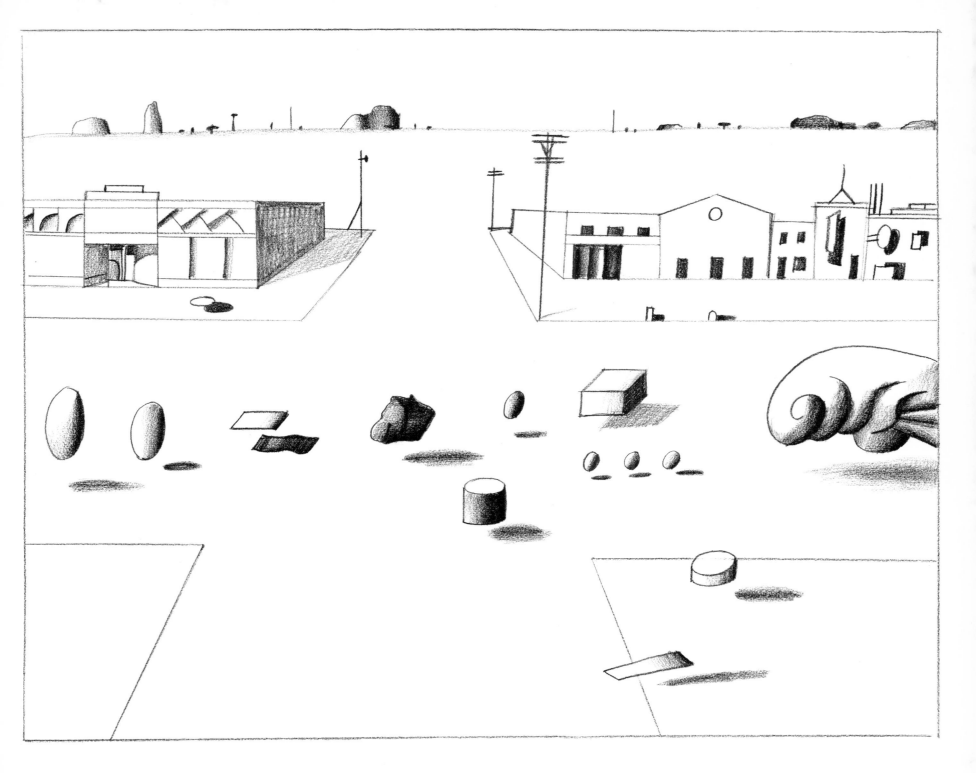

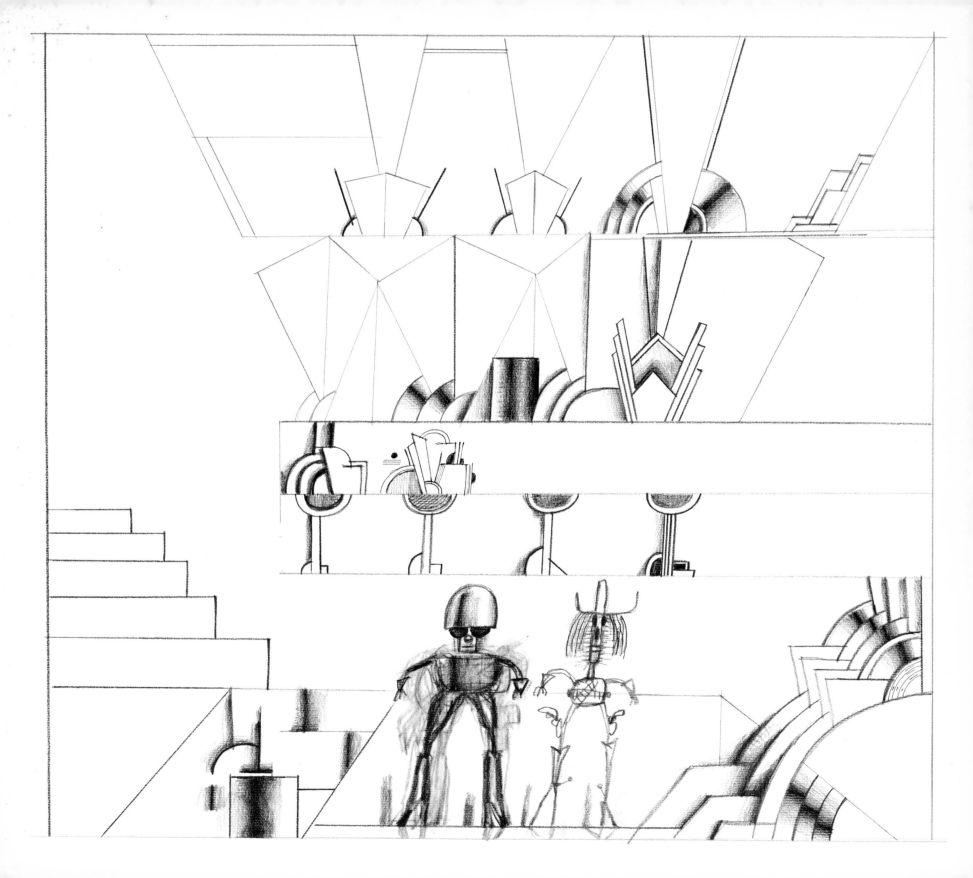

STEINBERG
1970

VIVAN
LAS
CADENAS

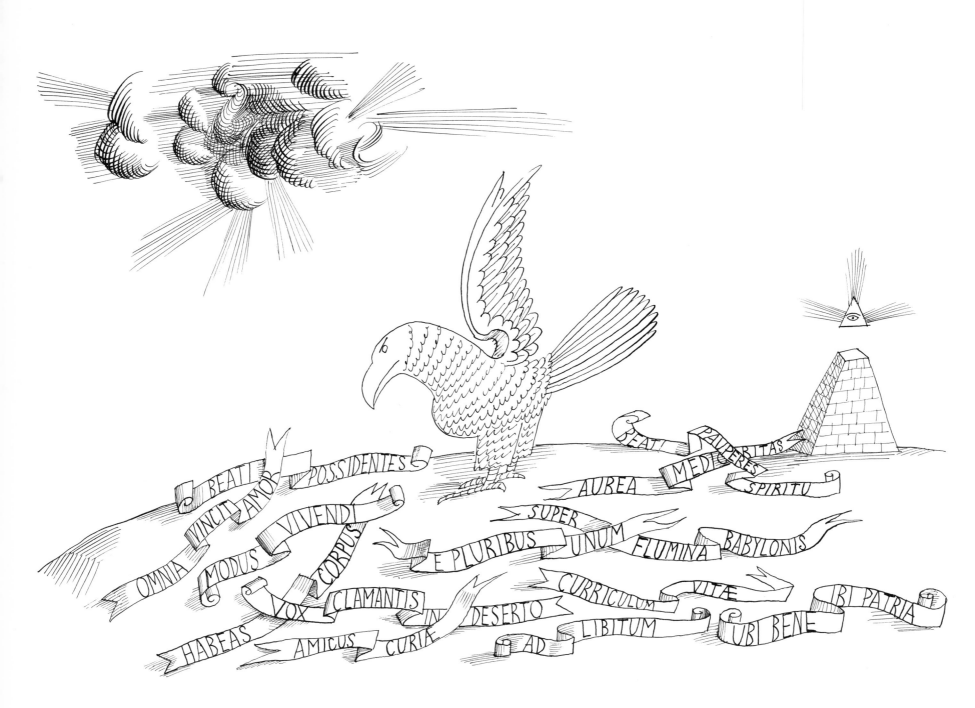

Cody

WYOMING

97914 sq. mi.

Laramie

Cheyenne

402 — Papeete TAHITI
425 — MARTINIQUE
589 — OAHU
640 — Honolulu ZANZIBAR
ALBANIA

10 632 —
3 275 — LAKE TITICACA
9 925 —
13 433 — SICILY HOLLAND
34 813 — CALABRIA

Taranto
BASILICATA CAMPANIA Napoli Roma
PUGLIA LAZIO
Bari ABRUZZI
7836 — NEW Newark
JERSEY
15944 — Atlantic City
97914 sq. mi. Zurich
SWITZERLAND

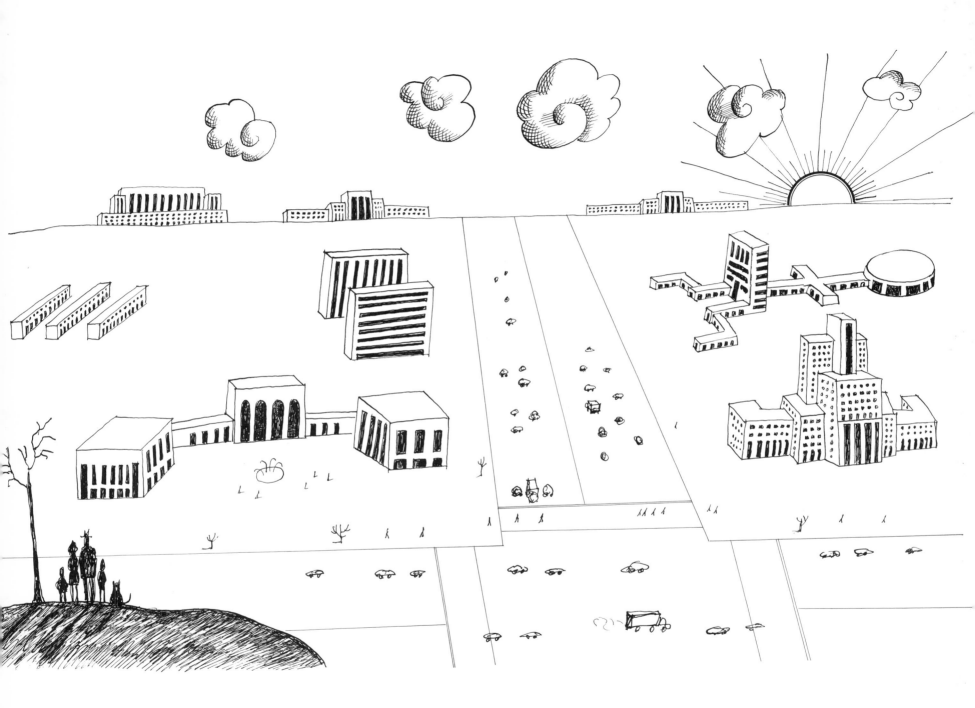

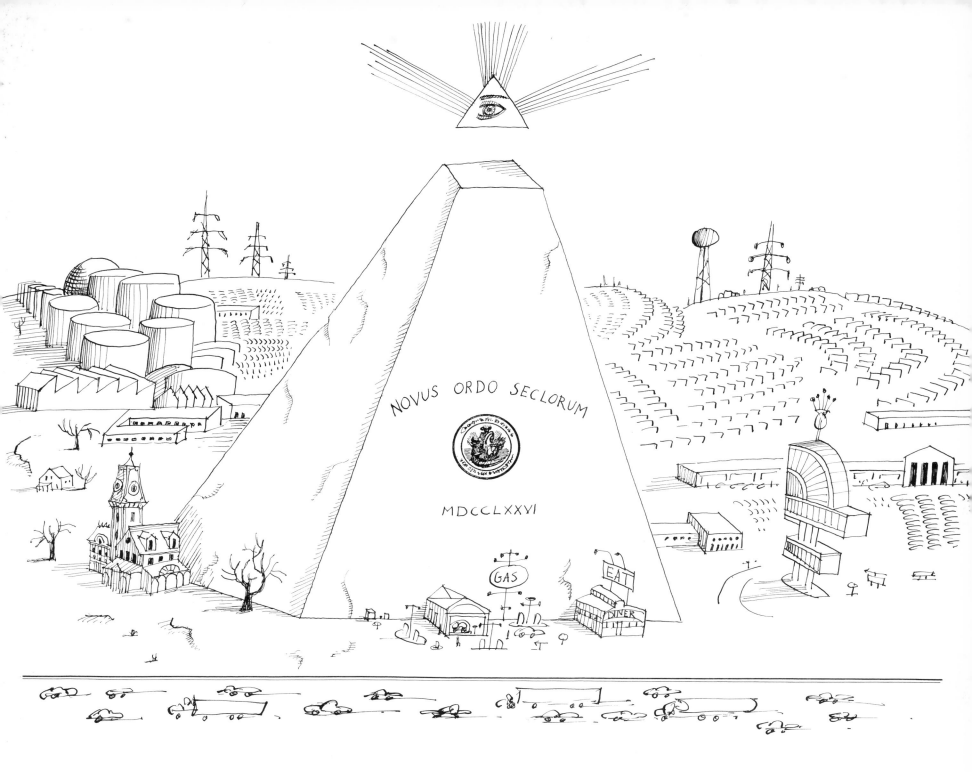

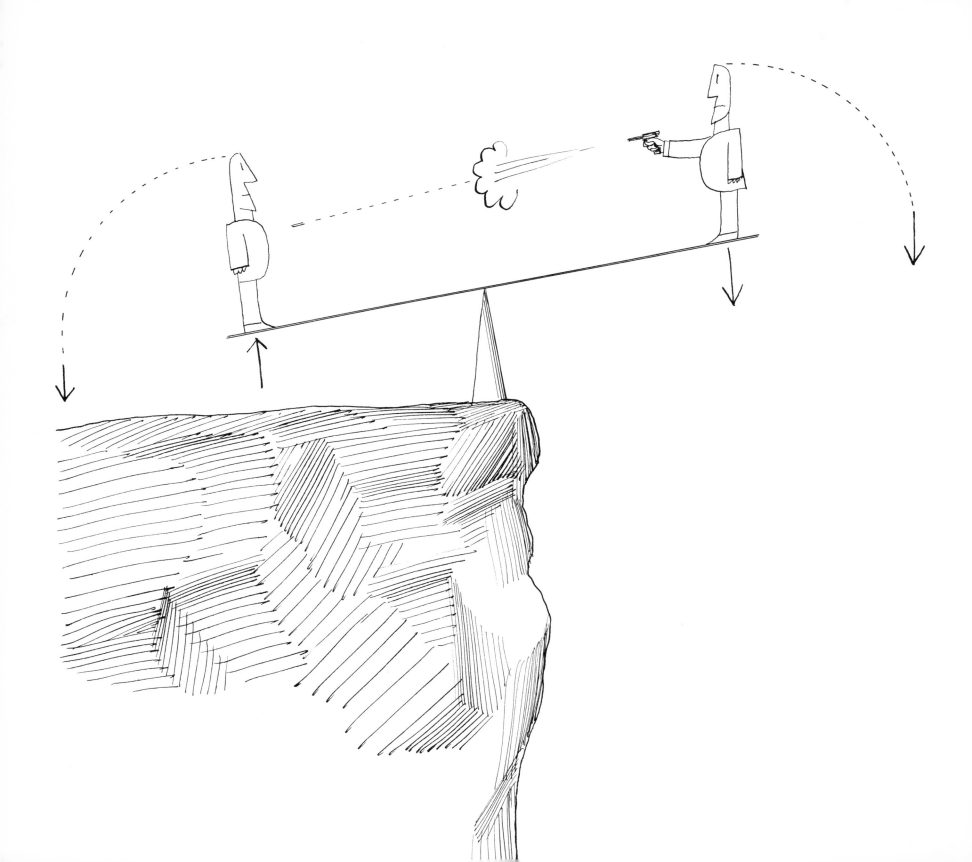

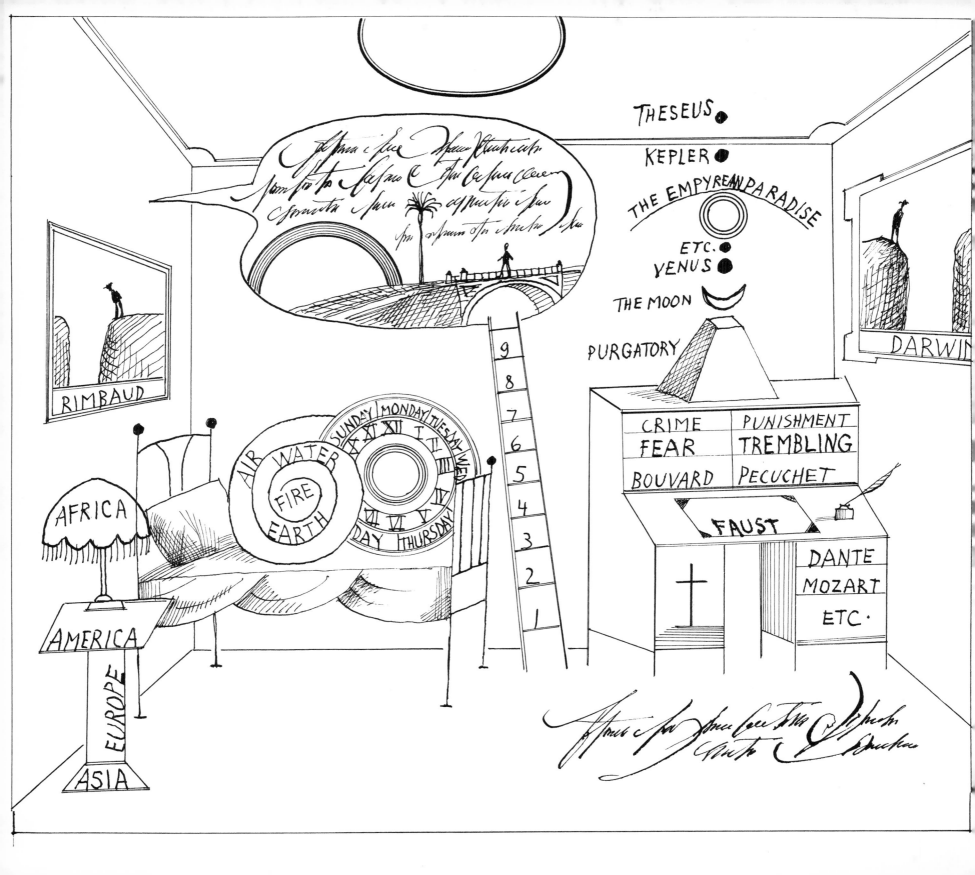

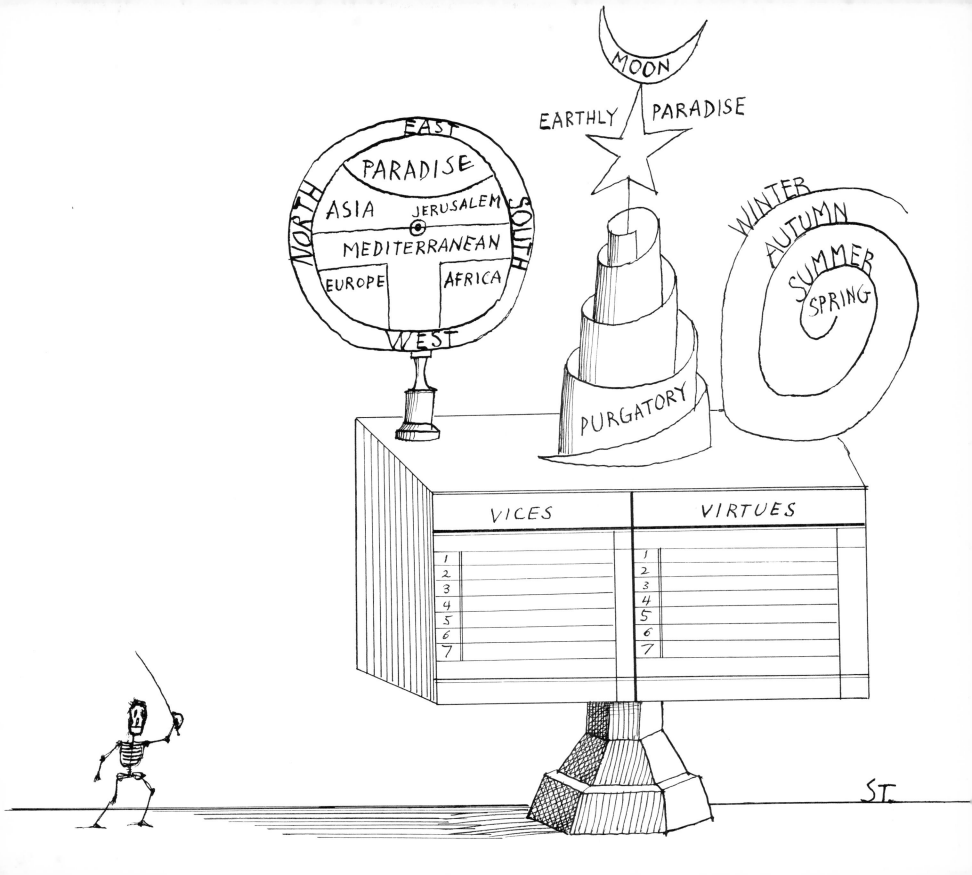

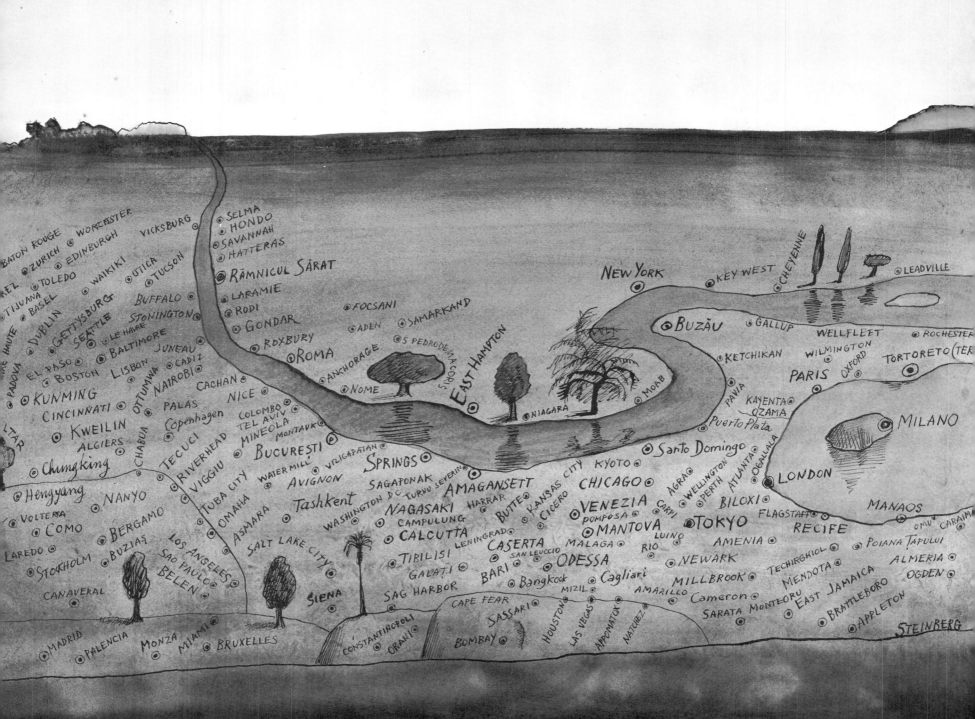

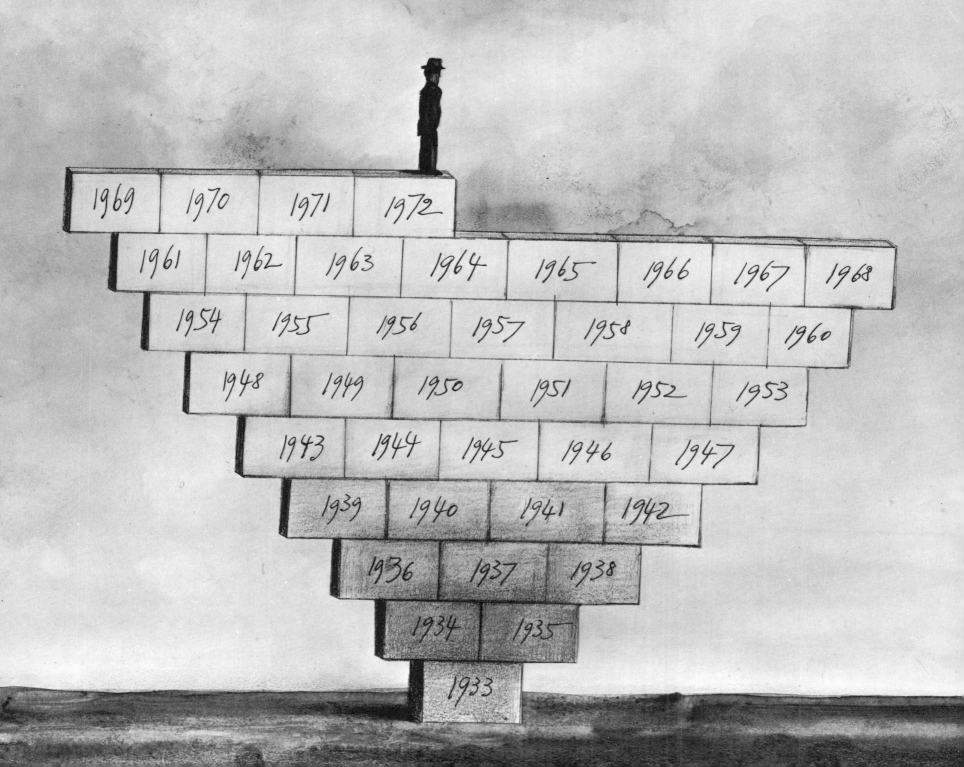

STEINBERG
TO BE
ARE WE?
I WAS
I SHALL
I WILL!
I AM
WE ARE
I would
I SHOULD

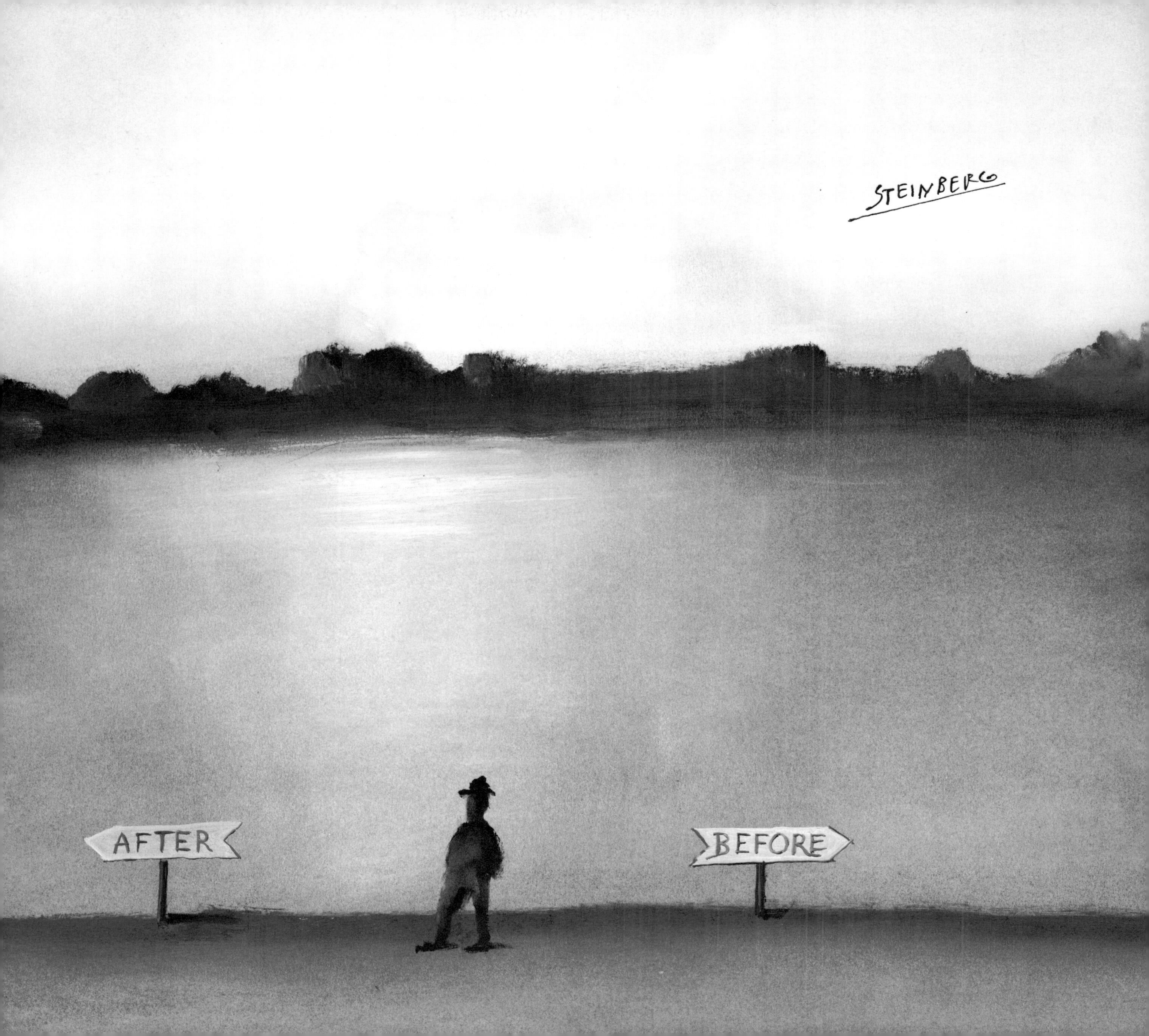
STEINBERG
AFTER
BEFORE

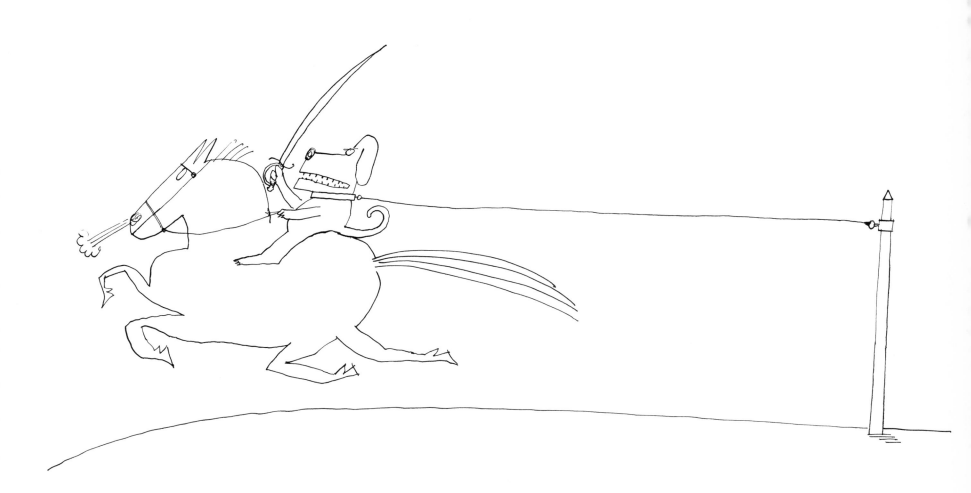

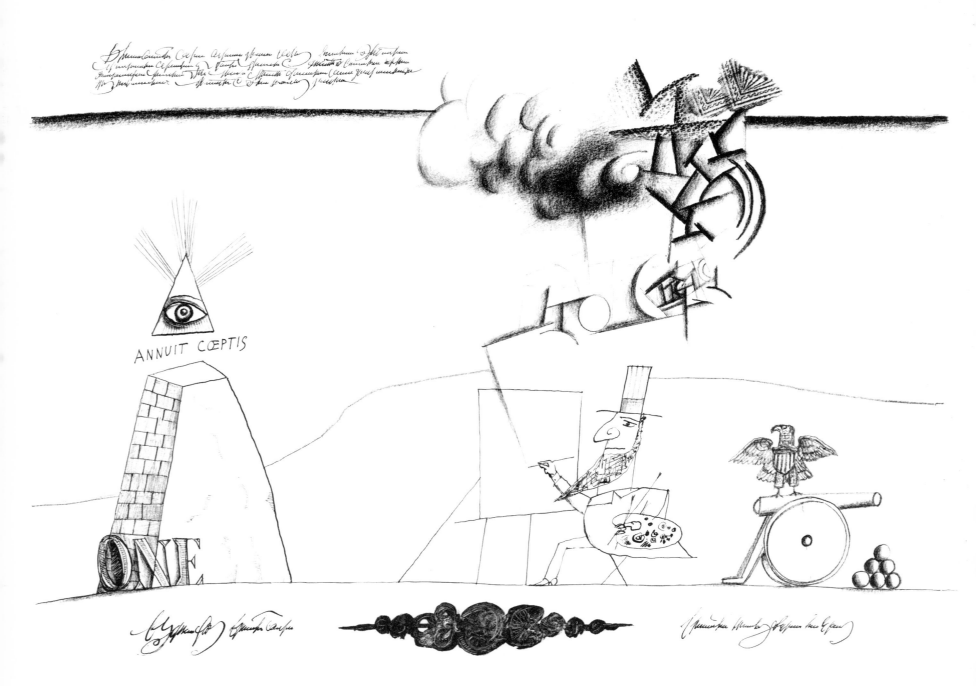

ANNUIT CŒPTIS

ONE